RUFUS' ROOAAR!

A BOOK BY JAMES NOVY

GW00865255

The illustrations in this book were hand drawn in pencil,
magic markers, and water color and digitally composited
using Adobe Illustrator, Photoshop, and Flash.

ISBN: 978-1-257-03662-2

For more fun with Rufus, go to:
www.RufusTheMonster.com

For
Ilana
&
Jacob

Rufus was a monster.

A very, very, BIG monster.

He was bigger than a house and WAY BIGGER
than you or me.

Rufus was one of the nicest monsters around. But to everyone else, he looked mean and ferocious.

His face was always stuck in a frown. He tried and tried and tried, but he just couldn't turn his frown into a smile.

Rufus was also very polite. He would always say things like, "Hello," or "Thank you very much."

But to everyone else, it always sounded like,

"RRRROOOOOAAAAARR!"

Needless to say, Rufus was a very sad and lonely monster.

One day, Rufus was terribly hungry. He looked all around and saw a BIG ice cream cone. "Yummy!" said Rufus.

But of course, it sounded like,

"RRRROOOOOAAAAARR!"

Rufus ran toward the ice cream cone as fast as he could. But every time Rufus ran, his arms, feet, and tail would crash into anything close by. "Sorry!" said Rufus.

But of course, it sounded like,

"RRRROOOOOAAAARR!"

Just as Rufus was about to eat his ice cream, he noticed that it had become really noisy. People were screaming, cars were honking, and sirens were sounding.

Rufus saw a group of people nearby and asked, "Excuse me. What's going on?"

But of course, when he said this, it sounded like,

"RRRROOOOOAAAAARR!"

So the people just screamed and ran away.

Suddenly, a group of policemen surrounded Rufus.
"Freeze!" they shouted, "Drop the ice cream
cone and put your hand and claw in the air!"

Rufus was really scared. He dropped the ice
cream cone and raised his arms. "I'm sorry,"
he said, "I didn't mean to do anything wrong."

But of course, to the policemen, it sounded like,

"RRRROOOOOAAAAARR!"

"Get him!" shouted the policemen.
Rufus became so frightened that he started to run away as fast as he could. The policemen hopped into their police cars and helicopters and chased after Rufus.

"I didn't mean to do anything wrong," shouted Rufus, "I'm sorry!"

Rufus found a quiet spot to hide in the park. He sat down and wondered why no one wanted to be near him and why the police were so mad at him. He felt really sad and lonely.

AND he was still terribly hungry.

All of a sudden, Rufus heard a tiny voice from below.

"Hello."

Standing next to Rufus was a little girl. "Sounds like you're hungry," she said, "I can hear your tummy rumbling." It was so calm and quiet that Rufus could hear his tummy rumbling too.

The little girl held her hand out to Rufus. "Here, you can have some of my ice cream if you'd like." Rufus looked at the little girl and paused for a moment. "It's OK," she said, "I won't bite."

Rufus gently took the ice cream cone from the little girl. He took the tiniest bite he could with his BIG, BIG teeth. The ice cream tasted soooo good!

"Do you feel better now?" asked the little girl. Rufus nodded and was just about to say "Thank you," when all of a sudden, the policemen appeared again in a big commotion.

"Be careful!" shouted the policemen to the little girl, "You're standing next to a mean and ferocious monster!"

"He's not mean and ferocious," said the little girl to the policemen, "He's just really hungry. Can't you hear his tummy rumbling?"

The policemen stopped and listened. It became so calm and quiet that they could hear Rufus' tummy rumbling too.

Then the policemen realized what had happened. They had looked at Rufus' frown and thought that he was mean. They had heard his "RRROOOAAARRR!" and thought that he was ferocious.

But Rufus wasn't mean or ferocious at all. It was just a BIG misunderstanding.

The policemen felt really bad. "We're sorry,"
they said, "We were wrong to chase after you.
Can you ever forgive us?"

Rufus nodded and said, "Yeah, it's OK."

But of course, it sounded like,

"RRRROOOOOAAAARR!"

The little girl and the policemen all laughed and laughed. At that moment, Rufus was the happiest he had ever been and he didn't feel lonely or sad anymore...

...and suddenly, Rufus' frown became a great BIG beautiful smile!

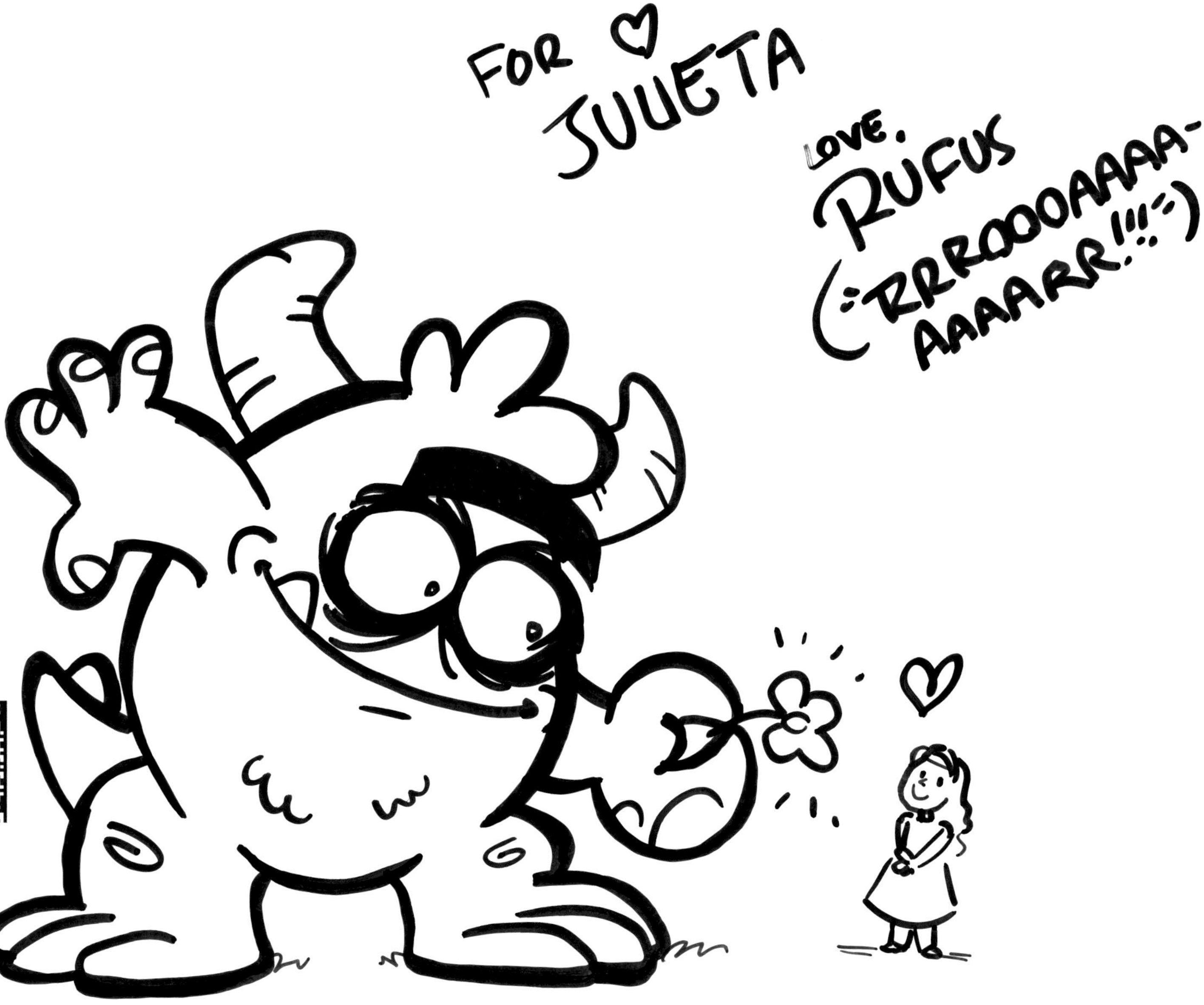
FOR ♡ JULIETA
LOVE, RUFUS
(:-RRROOOAAAA-AAAAARR!!!:-)

Page Count: 27-30

Due Date: Wednesday

Comment: 4/2/2014